Adieu: Love's Farewe

Akrati Sharma

www.draft2digital.com

Copyright

Table of Contents

Preface

Love's ethereal dance, in hearts it resides,
A kaleidoscope of emotions, it guides.
In its embrace, souls find solace and light,
A timeless symphony, pure and infinite.

In the realm of love, where emotions intertwine like melodies, there exist tales that transcend the ordinary, weaving a tapestry of profound connections and bittersweet farewells. "Adieu: Love's Farewell Symphony" invites you to embark on a journey through the pages of a story that unfolds like a timeless melody, resonating with the depths of human emotions.

In this tender and poignant tale penned by the talented Akrati Sharma, we are immersed in the lives of Siddharth and Arunima, two souls bound by a love that defies the boundaries of time and adversity. It is a tale of unexpected challenges and the resilience of the human spirit, where love confronts mortality and emerges stronger than ever.

As you turn the pages, be prepared to witness a love that knows no bounds—a love that refuses to be silenced, even in the face of life's cruelest tests. Through Akrati Sharma's evocative prose, you will experience the turmoil of emotions that both Siddharth and Arunima endure, their hearts entwined in a delicate dance between hope and despair.

"Adieu: Love's Farewell Symphony" delves into the depths of the human condition, exploring themes of sacrifice, resilience, and the enduring power of love. It challenges us to reflect on the preciousness of every moment and the transformative nature of love, even in the face of unimaginable pain.

Prepare to be swept away by the author's enchanting words as she crafts a symphony of emotions that will resonate with your heartstrings. You will be captivated by the characters' struggles and triumphs, as well as their unwavering determination to cherish the present and embrace the inevitable.

As you immerse yourself in this heartfelt story, allow yourself to be carried away by the melodies of love and loss, of strength and vulnerability. Akrati Sharma's exquisite storytelling will transport you to a world where love shines brightest in the darkest moments—a world where the power of the human spirit knows no boundaries.

So, dear reader, let the music of "Adieu: Love's Farewell Symphony" resonate within you, drawing forth the tears and emotions that lie dormant in the depths of your soul. May you find solace and inspiration in the profound journey of Siddharth and Arunima—a tale that will leave an indelible mark on your heart long after you have turned the final page.

With each word penned by Akrati Sharma, let us embark on this unforgettable journey— an ode to love, to life, and to the beauty of bidding adieu.

Enjoy the symphony.

Chapter 1

In New City

Their gazes lingered, desperately holding on until their connection was inevitably severed. And in that moment, a wave of sorrow washed over her, crashing against the dam she had carefully constructed to contain her emotions for so long.

Siddharth's departure unleashed a torrent of tears, releasing the pent-up feelings she had suppressed with unwavering strength. Siddharth and Arunima had been inseparable best friends for the past three years, their bond unbreakable.

As Siddharth faded from view, the passing of years, months, and days flashed before her eyes, a montage of memories that seemed to both comfort and torment her.

The day they first met, the arguments they overcame, the shared indulgence in late-night ice creams, all rushed through her mind as she made her way home, carrying the weight of their parting on her shoulders.

"What? Delhi? Are you out of your mind? You're actually saying you're leaving Mumbai... Are you crazy?" The words erupted from her with a mix of disbelief and frustration, punctuated by the sharp edges of her voice. Siddharth had just delivered the news, and Arunima couldn't help but react with an outburst of emotions.

He had managed to secure admission in one of the most prestigious media colleges in the country, but the thought of their imminent separation weighed heavily on her heart. Deep down, amidst the twinge of sadness, Arunima found a glimmer of happiness for Siddharth's promising future.

******

The new city embraced Siddharth with open arms, its vibrant energy fueling his excitement. The unfamiliar corridors of the college echoed with the buzz of fresh beginnings, and each face he encountered held a story waiting to be discovered.

Meanwhile, in Mumbai, Arunima embarked on a new journey of her own, diligently attending coaching classes to prepare for the challenging civil services examination.

Their lives took on a busy rhythm, with days slipping by in a whirlwind of responsibilities. However, amidst the chaos, they always found solace in the quiet hours of the night.

With unwavering dedication, they would carve out at least an hour to share their stories, recounting the intricacies of their respective days, bridging the physical distance between them with the power of their conversations.

As Arunima's crucial exams drew near, she immersed herself in relentless study sessions, determined to conquer the upcoming prelims. On one particular evening,

Siddharth reached out, eagerly seeking to connect with her. However, to his surprise, there was no answer to his call. Hours passed, and he persistently attempted to reach her, growing increasingly anxious with every unanswered ring.

Just as he was beginning to lose hope, a flicker of relief illuminated his mobile screen as Arunima's number finally appeared, signaling her response.

"Siddharth... I'm really sorry, I couldn't answer your call," Arunima's voice filled with regret as she spoke.

"Where were you, Arunima...? Are you alright? I was genuinely worried," Siddharth's concern echoed in his words.

"Yeah, I'm fine. I was actually at my friend's place for some study time. I completely forgot to take my phone along," Arunima explained, a hint of apology in her tone.

"Which friend? I mean, are you part of a study group?" Siddharth inquired, his voice carrying a tinge of curiosity.

"Not exactly a study group. It's just the two of us. Gaurav lives nearby and he's also preparing for the Civil Services exam. We decided to study together. Plus, he has attempted it before, so his experience comes in handy," Arunima clarified, hoping to ease any concerns.

"Okay..." Siddharth's response was tinged with a touch of coldness, his emotions guarded.

As time passed, their conversations grew shorter in duration, even though they continued to maintain contact. Both Siddharth and Arunima found themselves caught up in the demands of their respective pursuits. Siddharth's own examinations loomed closer, and he was acutely aware of the immense challenge that lay ahead in cracking the tough nut of the Civil Services Examination.

"I have something to ask you, Arunima," Siddharth's voice trembled with a hint of uncertainty during their customary call.

"Of course, Siddharth. What is it?" Arunima responded, in an attentive and curious tone of voice.

"Well... Actually..." Siddharth paused, collecting his thoughts before continuing. "How are your preparations coming along? With the exams right around the corner, I can't help but wonder."

"I believe I've put in considerable effort, Siddharth. Only time will tell how it pays off," Arunima shared, giving him an update on her progress. "Is that what you wanted to ask me? I feel like I've been keeping you informed every day."

"Yes, I know. It's just that there's something else on my mind. However, I thought it best to wait until after your exams.

We can discuss it later," Siddharth explained, a touch of patience resonating in his voice.

"Alright, Siddharth. I'll patiently await our conversation. Whenever you feel ready to talk about it, I'll be here," Arunima responded, her words filled with understanding and assurance.

As the day of the exams arrived, Siddharth sent his heartfelt wishes and good luck to Arunima. With anticipation building up within him, he eagerly waited for her call. Siddharth understood the immense significance of clearing the prelims for Arunima, and he hoped that her hard work would bear fruit.

Finally, Arunima's call came, and even before she spoke, her voice carried a hint of the outcome. It was evident that the exam had gone well for her. She had tackled the questions with confidence and fairness, leaving no stone unturned. However, the unpredictable nature of competitive exams lingered in her mind.

Despite feeling satisfied with her performance, Arunima maintained a cautious optimism, keeping her fingers crossed, aware that the final results were still uncertain.

Siddharth made his customary call to Arunima during their usual late-night time slot. However, he encountered a busy tone when he attempted to reach her. Undeterred, he tried again after 15 minutes, only to find the line still engaged.

"Your phone was busy, Arunima..." he remarked when she finally called back after approximately half an hour.

The use of her full name, Arunima, instead of his usual endearment, Aru, hinted at Siddharth's mild surprise.

"Yes, I was talking to Gaurav," Arunima explained. "I had visited his place after the exam, but he wasn't home at the time. So, he called me back. You know what... his exams didn't go as well as he had hoped, and he was feeling a bit down. I was just trying to lift his spirits and offer some support. That's why the call ended up lasting so long."

Siddharth's silence lingered for a moment, causing a hint of concern in Arunima's voice.

"Siddharth... Are you there?" Arunima asked, a genuine worry obvious in her voice.

"Yeah... I'm here. Just listening," Siddharth responded, his tone subdued.

"Are you alright? What's going on, Siddharth?" Arunima pressed, her concern growing more evident.

"It's nothing... I don't know. I'm just not feeling good," Siddharth confessed, his words heavy with unspoken emotions.

"Not feeling good about what?" Arunima asked softly to know about his state of mind.

"Will you answer a question for me?" Siddharth said with uncertainty.

"Yes, of course," Arunima assured him, ready to provide the support he needed.

"Arunima... are you and Gaurav in a kind of relationship?" Siddharth's words brought an obvious laughter from Arunima's side.

"Siddharth..." Arunima's voice trembled with surprise and disbelief, struggling to comprehend the sudden question.

"I need to know, Arunima. It's just that every time we talk, Gaurav's name comes up. Your concern for his career, your close proximity in the neighborhood, studying together... Are you two involved romantically?" Siddharth could not hide his worries anymore so he asked everything openly.

The unexpected inquiry from Siddharth caught Arunima off guard, leaving her momentarily speechless. Their friendship had always been strong and open, and such questions had never arisen before. She just wondered that so much had changed between them in a short time period.

"Gaurav and I are just family friends, Siddharth," Arunima finally responded, her voice carrying a mix of emotions. "We connect for studies because of our shared goals. If ever I were to be involved with someone romantically, you would be the first person to know. You needn't ask me... You are my best friend, dear."

Silence settled between them, leaving Siddharth with his thoughts.

"Siddharth... is there something else on your mind?" Arunima gently probed, sensing his inner turmoil.

"I don't know... It's just this feeling that I need to talk to you about something," Siddharth confessed, his voice tinged with frustration.

"About what?" Arunima inquired very patiently.

"I don't know..." Siddharth's irritation was palpable, his uncertainty overshadowing his ability to articulate his thoughts.

Arunima chose to remain silent, allowing Siddharth the space to gather his words and express himself when he felt ready.

Siddharth continued, his voice carrying a hint of vulnerability. "I haven't been feeling well for the past few days. Maybe it's because we haven't had much time to talk. Honestly, I'm not sure."

"Hmm... How are things going in your college? How did your exams go?" Arunima inquired, trying to shift the focus to brighter topics.

"It was only and internal exam, and everything was fine," Siddharth replied with a kind of unease.

"Okay... Anything new happening there? Any interesting gossip or buzz in your college?" Arunima asked just to make him happy again.

"No, nothing like that," Siddharth responded, his voice lacking enthusiasm.

"What are you saying? Your city is known for its vibrant atmosphere and beautiful girls. You mean to tell me you couldn't find anyone for yourself?" Arunima teased, letting out a giggle in an effort to bring a smile to Siddharth's face.

"Arunima... I'm really not in the mood for such jokes," Siddharth responded, his tone serious. He paused for a moment before continuing. "By the way, there is a girl and she proposed to me the day before."

"Oh... now I understand why you've been feeling off lately," Arunima remarked playfully. "So, did you accept her proposal? Seems like love is in the air... ahem, ahem."

"Shut up, Arunima... I actually rejected her," Siddharth replied, his voice tinged with a hint of frustration.

"Really? But why? Wasn't she your type?" Arunima inquired, genuinely curious about Siddharth's decision.

"Arunima, I don't want to discuss this any further. I just shared it with you, but it's not that important," Siddharth stated, his words carrying a sense of finality.

After their conversation, they eventually hung up, but Arunima couldn't shake off the feeling that she hadn't been able to uplift Siddharth's spirits or comprehend the underlying cause of his distress.

Siddharth, true to his nature, retreated into silence for the next few days, a pattern he often followed after serious arguments. However, this time, there was no discernible reason for their disconnect—no fights, no arguments.

The absence of any identifiable trigger left Arunima puzzled and concerned. She couldn't help but wonder what could be weighing heavily on Siddharth's mind, causing him to withdraw into silence.

The unexplained silence between them stretched on, leaving Arunima yearning for answers and longing to bridge the growing emotional gap between them.

Arunima's words flowed freely during their daily conversations, with Siddharth often taking on a more passive role.

Chapter 2

After the Festivities

The following week, Arunima embarked on a journey to Bangalore to attend her cousin's wedding. She had informed Siddharth beforehand that she would be away for a couple of weeks and wouldn't be able to engage in their daily conversations.

Initially, they exchanged messages, attempting to stay connected despite the distance. However, as Arunima became immersed in the wedding rituals and family celebrations, her ability to actively respond to Siddharth's messages diminished. Her focus shifted to the joyous festivities, leaving little room for consistent communication with Siddharth.

After five days of being occupied with the wedding celebrations, Arunima found a moment to excuse herself for a walk in the garden post-dinner. Seizing the opportunity, she called Siddharth, and to her surprise, he answered immediately, as if eagerly anticipating her call.

"Hey, hero! What's up?" Arunima greeted him cheerfully.

"Too busy, right?" Siddharth responded, his tone laced with sarcasm.

"Yeah, Siddharth... The whole family is here, and I simply couldn't find any time to call. I'm really sorry," Arunima explained.

"It's okay. I understand. But at least you could reply to my messages..." Siddharth expressed his frustration.

Arunima explained that she couldn't bring her phone with her during the rituals. However, she assured her dear one that she would check and respond to all the messages whenever she had the opportunity. Additionally, she believed that this separation might provide them with some valuable time apart. Arunima's voice faded as she finished speaking.

"Time for what, Arunima?" Siddharth inquired, his tone tinged with curiosity.

"I don't know, Siddharth... You've seemed upset for a while, and I thought you might need some time or maybe some space. And being away seemed like an opportunity for that," Arunima explained.

"You had given me enough time during your exams, Arunima. I don't need any more time. When are you coming back?" Siddharth questioned, his concern evident.

"Siddharth... actually, I think my stay here might be extended," Arunima revealed.

"What? You said you would be back in two weeks," Siddharth expressed his surprise.

"Due to my extended absence, my family is urging me to prolong my stay here. Besides, my exams are over, and there isn't much for me to do in Mumbai right now," Arunima elaborated.

"So, how long will it be?" Siddharth inquired, his voice tinged with disappointment.

"Maybe I'll extend it by a week," Arunima responded.

"So, two more weeks to go, right?" Siddharth clarified.

"Yeah, kind of," Arunima reluctantly confirmed.

"Cool... enjoy," Siddharth responded, though Arunima could sense his underlying unhappiness. "By the way, when are we talking next? After a week or directly after two weeks when you're back? I understand you must be busy with your family obligations and all!"

"Siddharth... don't be so sarcastic. I will try to call you, but it's really challenging for me to manage everything here," Arunima explained.

Siddharth expressed surprise, asking why Arunima was attempting to make phone calls if she was unable to carry her phone during the rituals.

"I said I will, Siddharth. And this is an important family function. I can't simply avoid it," Arunima responded, her tone slightly frustrated.

"And me... I have no importance in your life?" Siddharth's words held a tinge of disappointment.

"Siddharth, please... you're overreacting. This is my family we're talking about," Arunima pleaded.

"And friends mean nothing to you... right?" Siddharth's words carried a hint of hurt.

"It's not like that, Siddharth... What has happened to you? Why are you behaving this way? It's really getting to me. These past few weeks, you've been treating me as if I've committed some crime. Will you please tell me what's going on in your mind?" Arunima's voice rose as she almost yelled.

Siddharth remained silent, not uttering a single word. He knew Arunima was right. He had been treating her rudely without any valid reason. He couldn't fully comprehend his own feelings.

"Siddharth... okay, I'm sorry. I shouldn't have yelled at you. But can we please discuss what's wrong? Siddharth... please talk to me," Arunima pleaded when she found no response.

"Arunima... can we talk later?" Siddharth requested.

"Siddharth..."
Arunima's voice trailed off, expressing her disappointment.

"Please..." Siddharth's voice softened.

"Okay. Take care. And let me know when we can talk about this," Arunima reluctantly agreed.

"Hmm," Siddharth replied, and they hung up, leaving the conversation unresolved.

Chapter 3

Sleepless Night

Arunima couldn't sleep that night, her mind consumed by thoughts of Siddharth's behavior. She tried to recall their recent conversations, searching for a reason behind his frustration. Perhaps Siddharth was hiding something, maybe there was a family issue she wasn't aware of. Those thoughts raced through her mind as she slipped out into the garden, dialing his number at 2 am.

As expected, he answered promptly, indicating he was still awake.

"Hi Siddharth..."

"Arunima, why did you call so late?" he asked.

"Why are you still awake, Siddharth?" Arunima inquired.

"Can I ask you the same question?"

"Yes, of course... I couldn't sleep, and I was thinking about you. Can we talk now?"

"Yeah... okay."

"How are things at home?" Arunima asked, trying to make conversation.

"Fine. Nothing new," Siddharth replied.

"What about your parents?"

"They're doing well," he answered.

"And your college?"

"Are you calling me at this hour only to inquire about my life?" Siddharth interrupted, his tone conveying a slight irritation.

"I just wanted to..."

"Wanted to what? Arunima, I'm sorry for my behavior in the past few days. I don't even know the reason behind it. Everything in my life seems fine, but something has changed. I've made friends in Delhi, but I still feel incredibly lonely..." Siddharth's voice trailed off, revealing his inner turmoil.

He paused for a moment, and Arunima remained silent, allowing him to continue pouring out his feelings. "At first, I was filled with excitement about my new career, and I'm genuinely enjoying it. However, Arunima, I long to return. I miss our old days," Siddharth confessed, expressing his desire to reunite with past memories.

"And what will you do once you're back?" she asked, her voice filled with curiosity and concern.

"I'll be with you, at least," Siddharth replied, his voice tinged with longing.

"Siddharth, you want to return and be with me? Are you alright?" Arunima asked, her voice filled with surprise in response to his unexpected revelation.

"No, I'm not okay. I'm missing you terribly. I can't concentrate on my studies. Despite all the excitement around me, I can't fully enjoy it because you're constantly on my mind... I never thought I would go through this, but..."

"But what, Siddharth?" Arunima encouraged him to continue.

"Arunima... I think... I think..." Siddharth hesitated, his words hanging in the air.

"I think?" Arunima pressed, her heart pounding.

"I think I love you, Arunima," Siddharth finally confessed, his voice filled with both vulnerability and hope.

"Siddharth..." she sighed, overwhelmed by his declaration.

"Arunima, it's completely okay if you don't feel the same way. I just wanted to tell you so that I feel better. I've been trying to gather the courage to say this for a while now, but every time, I end up feeling frustrated. I just couldn't..."

"What stopped you, Siddharth?" Arunima interrupted, her voice filled with tenderness.

"I thought you might become angry with me. I didn't want to lose my best friend," Siddharth admitted, his voice laced with fear.

"You silly fool... You'll never lose me as a friend, no matter what happens. By the way..."

Arunima stumbled, struggling to find the right words to continue.

"By the way, what, Arunima?" Siddharth asked, anticipation evident in his voice.

"Actually... I think I was waiting for this," she confessed, her voice filled with a mix of excitement and relief.

"Arunima?!" Siddharth was shocked. He had never considered the possibility of them being more than friends.

"Siddharth... I've been waiting for the past two years. I was simply too afraid to confess my feelings to you. I always believed you only saw me as a friend, so I didn't want to risk jeopardizing our relationship," Arunima revealed, her voice quivering with emotional vulnerability.

"Yeah, I did see you as a friend only. And I wouldn't have realized my true feelings if I hadn't been away from you. I've shared every moment with you over calls, but many times, I've wished you were by my side. I long for the moments we shared, the arguments we had, and the playful pranks I used to play on you. These small things now seem so significant to me, Arunima," Siddharth confessed, his voice filled with nostalgia.

They spoke their hearts out, completely unaware of the passage of time. As dawn broke, signaling a fresh morning, love was in the air. Arunima quietly slipped back into her room before anyone could notice her. Now, she no longer wanted to prolong her stay in

Bangalore. She yearned to return to Mumbai, to start a new life with Siddharth by her side.

Calls continued, but now with a newfound romantic undertone. Their conversations shifted from friendly chats to passionate exchanges. They would talk for hours into the night, exploring the depths of their love.

Despite being best friends for years, discovering their romantic connection added a spark to their relationship. Each passing day only intensified their love for each other.

One lazy Sunday morning, wrapped in a cozy blanket, Arunima was talking to Siddharth. She expressed her longing to meet him and her impatience to wait any longer. However, she also wanted him to focus on his semester exams so that they could have uninterrupted quality time together. When they last saw each other, they were just friends.

Arunima sighed wistfully, her voice filled with yearning, and expressed, "I wish you were here with me right now..." Her words trailed off as she closed her eyes, lost in the depth of her longing.

"You lazy creature, even if I were there, you wouldn't get out of your blanket to meet me, would you?" Siddharth teased, his affectionate tone evident.

"Hey, Mr. You're underestimating me, okay?" Arunima retorted, playfully narrowing her eyes.

"Really?" Siddharth challenged.

"Of course! You come and see for yourself," Arunima confidently replied.

"Alright then, get out of bed, get ready, and come out!" Siddharth declared, his voice filled with excitement.

"What do you mean?" Arunima asked, taken aback by his sudden request.

"Silly one... Meet me at the designated Meeting Point in thirty minutes. It's non-negotiable," Siddharth instructed, his tone firm and resolute.

"Are you kidding me? And it's not even April Fools' Day," Arunima exclaimed, shocked and finding it hard to believe.

"Don't waste my time," Siddharth playfully chided her.

Unable to contain her excitement, Arunima leaped out of bed and hastily got ready. She rushed to the door but then quickly turned back to check herself in the mirror one last time. With a smile and a blown kiss to her reflection, she confidently stepped out, eager to meet Siddharth at their designated Meeting Point.

Chapter 4

Surprise

Arunima anxiously scanned the coffee shop's glass walls, hoping to catch a glimpse of Siddharth. However, her search yielded no sign of him. Growing increasingly concerned, she decided to call Siddharth for an update.

"Siddharth, where are you?" Arunima asked, her voice filled with concern.

Siddharth replied, questioning her in return, "Where are you, Arunima?"

"I'm at the Meeting Point," she responded, hoping to find reassurance.

He expressed his shock, saying, "Please don't tell me you're actually there."

Confused, Arunima asked, "What do you mean?"

Siddharth chuckled and said, "Sweetheart, I was just joking."

Arunima's voice trembled as she asked, "Are you serious, Siddharth?"

Siddharth's laughter softened, and he explained, "Hey, Arunima... How could I come today when we discussed yesterday that we would meet after my exams?" He laughed again, this time more gently.

Arunima fell silent, her disappointment palpable.

"Arunima... what happened? Please say something," Siddharth pleaded.

Arunima, trying to compose herself, replied, "It's nothing. It's okay."

Siddharth, realizing the impact of his joke, apologized, "Arunima, I'm sorry, baby. I was just joking."

"It's okay, Siddharth... Can we talk later, please?" Arunima's voice quivered as tears filled her eyes. Although she was accustomed to his pranks, this time she had allowed herself to hope.

"Yes, honey, we can talk later. But before we hang up, let me tell you that you look beautiful in your blue salwar kameez," Siddharth complimented.

Arunima, her heart pounding, turned around in search of Siddharth but couldn't see him. Confused, she asked, "Siddharth, are you here?"

"And I never knew my Arunima could be so breathtaking. I had never witnessed this side of you before, Arunima. You look absolutely stunning with that perfectly coordinated bindi and bangles. Your flowing hair adds an enchanting touch," Siddharth continued, expressing his admiration for Arunima's appearance.

"Siddharth... where are you?" Arunima's restlessness grew.

"Turn around and take ten steps forward," Siddharth instructed gently.

Arunima followed his instructions cautiously and then came to a halt. "I'm not going any further, Siddharth."

"Please don't move, baby. Just turn around, please," Siddharth urged, his voice filled with anticipation.

Arunima turned around to see Siddharth standing right in front of her with a bouquet of roses. Her eyes widened with surprise and joy, and a smile spread across her face. She reached out to take the bouquet, feeling the softness of the petals against her fingertips.

Siddharth looked at her with admiration and love shining in his eyes. He took a step closer, his hand reaching out to gently caress her cheek. Arunima closed her eyes, savoring the touch and the warmth of his presence.

"You look absolutely stunning, Arunima," Siddharth whispered, his voice filled with sincerity. "I wanted to see you, to be with you, and to let you know how much you mean to me."

Arunima's heart raced with a mixture of emotions. She felt overwhelmed with happiness and a deep sense of connection. The realization of their mutual love enveloped them in a cocoon of warmth and tenderness.

Without uttering a word, they embraced each other tightly, cherishing the moment they had longed for. It was a silent celebration of their newfound love, a beautiful beginning to a journey they were about to embark on together.

As they embraced one another, it felt as if time had frozen. They transcended the boundaries of mere best friends and became soulmates, their connection deepened by the revelation of their true emotions.

Siddharth had planned to surprise her and spend some time together. He was supposed to leave the next day. Arunima was happy to see him but little sad about the trip being so short. A day wasn't enough for them. But Siddharth promised her to come back soon.

They spent the whole day together, creating beautiful memories and cherishing every moment. They roamed around the city, laughed, shared stories, and enjoyed each other's company. They dined at their favorite restaurants, indulged in some shopping, and even caught a romantic movie together, immersing themselves in the emotions of the story.

As the day drew to a close, the time came for Arunima to drop Siddharth off at the airport. It was a bittersweet moment, knowing that they had to part ways, at least for a little while. Arunima's emotions overwhelmed her, and tears streamed down her face uncontrollably.

Siddharth gently cupped her face with his hands, his touch offering comfort and reassurance. "Arunima, please don't cry, my love," he pleaded, his voice filled with tenderness. "I won't have the strength to leave if I see you in this state. Please, do your best to remain strong," Siddharth pleaded, urging Arunima to maintain her resilience.

Unable to contain her emotions, she buried her face in his chest, her tears soaking his shirt. He held her tightly, providing a sense of security and solace. He stayed by her side until her sobs subsided, his presence a source of strength.

Finally, he released her from his embrace and looked into her eyes, filled with love and determination. Her face was red, her eyes swollen from crying, but she was still the most beautiful person he had ever seen. Gently, he wiped away the strands of hair that were drenched in tears, his touch comforting and gentle.

"Sweets, my love, I promise you that I will be back soon," Siddharth whispered, his voice filled with sincerity. "Distance may separate us for a while, but our love will remain strong. We will get through this and be together again."

Arunima nodded, her trust in their love providing her with strength. Although their hearts ached at the prospect of being apart, they knew that their love would endure. With one last embrace and a lingering kiss, they bid each other farewell, holding onto the promise of a reunion in the near future.

Chapter 5

Achievement

With the exams approaching, Siddharth was caught up in the whirlwind of preparations, leaving him with little time to talk to Arunima. Despite the busy schedule, they managed to stay in touch through messages, offering each other support and encouragement.

Once the exams were finally over, relief did not come easily. The next phase involved interviews for internships, a mandatory requirement for first-year students.

Companies and agencies flooded in, seeking potential candidates. As expected,

Siddharth received an offer from one of India's top media agencies. Overjoyed by the news, he immediately called Arunima to share his success.

Arunima was elated for Siddharth's achievement and wanted to celebrate with him. However, there was a twist. The agency required him to join immediately for a two-month summer job.

This meant they would be unable to meet and celebrate his success in person. It was a bittersweet moment for both of them, realizing that their time together would be further delayed due to their individual commitments.

During the two months of Siddharth's internship, he found himself fully immersed in his work on a radio campaign. His responsibilities included assisting the campaign manager with research, findings, and the execution of the campaign.

This demanding role left Siddharth with little time for himself. Early mornings and late nights became the norm as he dedicated himself to his tasks. Amidst the hectic schedule, he could only find time to catch up with Arunima on weekends.

Meanwhile, the results for the Civil Services prelims were announced. Arunima eagerly purchased all the leading newspapers that were expected to publish the results. With her admit card in hand, she carefully scanned through the result page, reading it from top to bottom, bottom to top, left to right, and right to left.

Her eyes stopped at one particular number: AGE...012. Overwhelmed with joy, she couldn't contain her excitement and let out a scream, jumping around the house. She checked the result multiple times, still unable to believe her eyes. She had successfully cleared the first round.

Filled with exhilaration, Arunima immediately called Siddharth to share her news. However, he disconnected her call, leaving her disappointed. Soon after, a message from Siddharth appeared on her phone, explaining his busyness.

"Lil busy sweets. Call you later," his message read.

Not discouraged, Arunima replied, "No problem. I'll be waiting."

Arunima patiently waited for the entire day, hoping to receive a call from Siddharth. However, no call came. At one point, she even picked up her phone to redial his number but decided against it, not wanting to disturb him.

She knew that Siddharth was occupied with preparing for the launch of his campaign, which was scheduled in just two days. He had been working tirelessly, spending nights in the office and neglecting proper meals. Despite their lack of communication, Arunima kept track of his launch dates.

Finally, after two days, Arunima received a call from Siddharth. "Hi Siddharth," she greeted him.

"Hey Arunima. Sorry, dear. I was too busy to call or message. You won't believe it, but we successfully launched the campaign, and the response has been overwhelming. I'm so happy right now. I wish you were here so we could celebrate together," he exclaimed with excitement.

"Congratulations! That's fantastic news! I'm really happy for you," Arunima replied, genuinely sharing in his joy.

Siddharth continued sharing the details of his eventful week, describing how he received recognition and appreciation from his seniors. His passion and dedication towards his work were evident in his words. However, he suddenly paused, realizing that he had been speaking for the past 15 minutes without giving Arunima a chance to say anything.

Apologizing, Siddharth said, "Hey, I'm sorry, baby. You wanted to say something. Please tell me."

Arunima responded in a cold voice, "No problem, Siddharth. It's not a big deal. I just wanted to share that my results were out."

Sensing the shift in Arunima's tone, Siddharth swiftly picked up on her diminishing excitement. He promptly replied, "So... I gather it's good news then? Can I offer my congratulations?"

A small smile appeared on Arunima's face as she replied, "Yeah."

"Wow, Arunima! That's amazing news! I'm so happy for you," Siddharth exclaimed, genuinely excited. Getting through the Civil Services Prelims on her first attempt was a significant achievement, even though the main entrance test was yet to be faced.

"Thanks, Siddharth," Arunima replied.

"Hey, Arunima. What's going on? You don't sound too happy. Is everything okay?" Siddharth asked, picking up on her subdued voice.

"Yeah, of course, I'm happy, Siddharth. But it was just the prelims. The main exam is still ahead," Arunima replied.

"I understand, but I have complete confidence that you'll overcome that as well. You're a champion, my dear," Siddharth attempted to uplift Arunima's spirits. "Is there anything else, Arunima? Anything you'd like to share with me?"

"No, Siddharth. There's nothing else," she responded.

"Okay, I believe you. By the way, did I talk too much? I got carried away with excitement..." Siddharth trailed off.

"I understand, Siddharth, and I truly am happy for you," Arunima interrupted.

"Hmm. So, what's new on your end? It's been a while since we had a proper conversation," Siddharth asked.

"I know. I've joined classes for the main exam," Arunima replied.

"Hmm. So, once again, my darling will be busy and have no time for me," he playfully complained like a child.

They continued their conversation, but Siddharth couldn't shake off the feeling of tension between them. He was aware that he hadn't been able to devote enough time to Arunima, and he felt a sense of guilt weighing on him. However, his demanding work kept him occupied throughout the duration, leaving little room for personal commitments.

And just when he finally managed to find some time, Arunima became engrossed in her own exam preparations, further complicating their schedules.

Chapter 6

Distance

Siddharth could sense the distance growing between them. Despite Arunima's exams being over, their communication remained minimal. Siddharth became the sole initiator of their conversations, as Arunima seemed to avoid reaching out to him. Even when he called, she responded only to his direct questions, avoiding any further conversation.

Feeling concerned, Siddharth finally mustered the courage to address the issue. "Arunima, is everything okay?" he asked one day.

"Yeah, why? What happened?" she replied, her tone guarded.

"I can't help but notice that you've been distant. You seem to be avoiding me," Siddharth expressed his concerns.

"No, it's nothing like that," Arunima quickly dismissed.

"Then what is it, Arunima? I can sense that something is bothering you," Siddharth pressed on.

"I'm fine, really," Arunima insisted, her response lacking the conviction to convince him otherwise.

Siddharth could sense the coldness and sadness in Arunima's voice, but despite his attempts to probe further, she denied feeling low or upset. However, her behavior spoke otherwise.

She no longer expressed the desire to see him and didn't even suggest meeting up when they both had relatively more free time from their studies. Sensing the growing distance, Siddharth decided to ask her directly if they could meet.

"Would you like to come to Delhi, my dear?" Siddharth proposed.

"What for?" Arunima's response came off as rude.

"I just wanted to see you, dear. Or else, I can come to meet you. Maybe next week,"

Siddharth suggested, not waiting for her answer.

"No, Siddharth. It's okay. Finish your studies first. We can meet later," Arunima replied, seemingly avoiding the idea.

"Baby, my exams are in three months, and I'm not currently working on any project. I think I would be able to manage," Siddharth reasoned.

"But I'm a little busy next week. I'll let you know when I'm free," Arunima evaded, further avoiding the idea of meeting him.

Siddharth couldn't understand the reason behind Arunima's reluctance to meet him. Despite his efforts to make amends and bridge the distance, she seemed to be acting unreasonably.

Chapter 7

Glimpses of Sorrow

The doorbell rang, jolting Arunima out of her state of mind. She reluctantly got out of bed and opened the door, only to be shocked by who stood before her.

"Hey...surprise...se," Siddharth exclaimed, giving her a tight hug.

Arunima stood there in silence, her emotions conflicting within her.

Siddharth eventually released her from his embrace and looked at her expectantly.

"Hi Siddharth. It's a pleasant surprise," she managed to say, but her smile lacked its usual warmth. Siddharth observed her closely. He noticed that she had become fairer and slimmer since they last saw each other.

"So...someone has turned fair and lovely...ahem ahem...is this love?" Siddharth playfully teased, accompanied by a wink.

Arunima forced another smile and met his gaze.

"Arunima...I feel like you're not truly happy to see me here," Siddharth remarked, sensing her true emotions.

"It's not what you think, Siddharth. I truly am happy to see you. It's a delightful surprise," she responded, making an effort to regain her smile.

"It seems more like a shock, to be honest," Siddharth taunted, recognizing her hesitance. Arunima remained silent and took a step back, allowing him to enter the house.

Siddharth made himself comfortable in the drawing room, taking in the familiar surroundings adorned with framed photographs on the walls. The pictures captured moments of joy, featuring their college days, family, friends, and parties. One particular photo caught Siddharth's attention— a snapshot of Arunima, the tomboy he had known, and he couldn't help but smile at the transformation she had undergone, blossoming into a woman.

As he immersed himself in his thoughts, Arunima's voice broke the silence.

"Siddharth..." she called softly, offering him a glass of water.

"Thanks," he replied, accepting the glass and settling down on the sofa.

He gestured for Arunima to sit beside him, and she placed the tray on the center table before taking a seat on the sofa, maintaining a noticeable distance. Siddharth, sensing her discomfort, placed his glass on the table and inched closer to her.

Taking her hand gently, he covered it with both of his and looked into her eyes. Arunima's uneasiness was palpable.

"Sweets, I know there's something you're keeping from me," Siddharth said softly. "I couldn't convince you to talk about it over the phone, so I'm here now."

"Siddharth, I assure you, I'm not hiding anything. There's nothing..." Arunima began, but Siddharth interrupted her by placing his index finger gently on her lips, silencing her words.

Siddharth's heart sank as he heard Arunima's words. The realization of her developing feelings for someone else hit him hard. He took a deep breath to compose himself before responding.

"I see," Siddharth said, his voice strained. "I understand that you needed support during those times, and I deeply regret not being there for you. I'm truly sorry, Arunima."

Arunima looked at him, her eyes filled with a mix of sadness and guilt.

"Siddharth, I never meant for this to happen. It's just that Saurabh was there for me when I needed someone. I don't want to hurt you, but I have to be honest with myself."

Siddharth nodded, trying to hold back his emotions. "I appreciate your honesty, Arunima. If you believe that being with Saurabh will make you happier, then I won't hold you back."

Tears welled up in Arunima's eyes as she reached out to hold Siddharth's hand.

"Siddharth, you are such a wonderful person, and I'm so sorry for hurting you like this."

Siddharth smiled sadly and gently withdrew his hand from her grasp. "It's alright, Arunima. Sometimes, things don't go as we expect. I just want you to be happy, even if it means letting you go."

Silence hung in the air as they both sat there, the weight of their unfulfilled love lingering between them.

Siddharth was left speechless, unable to comprehend Arunima's words. His eyes filled with tears as he held her arms tightly, gazing deeply into her eyes.

"Arunima... This can't be real. You're joking, right? You can't be serious... Please tell me this is all a lie, a cruel act. You can't be doing this to me," Siddharth said, his voice trembling with disbelief. His body shook with the intensity of his emotions as he desperately sought an alternative explanation.

Arunima's trembling form and tears streaming down her face confirmed the painful truth. Slowly, she released herself from his grasp, and her words pierced through Siddharth's heart.

"I'm sorry, Siddharth, but it's true. I can't deny it any longer. I truly am sorry," Arunima replied, her voice filled with regret and sorrow.

Siddharth's world crumbled before his eyes as he struggled to accept the reality of the situation. He felt a profound sense of loss and a deep ache within his soul.

Chapter 8

Tracking Her

Resting on a park bench, Siddharth longed for the torment to be a mere figment of his imagination. Regrettably, it was an unwelcome reality that unfolded before him. Fixated on the tree above him, his gaze remained fixed as the wind gently stirred the rustling leaves.

Emptiness consumed him, overpowering his desire to shed tears. The urge to question Arunima about her motivations weighed heavily upon him, yet words eluded him. His mind felt void, a vast expanse of unanswered queries. Amidst the anguish, a small part of his heart whispered a consoling refrain, insisting, "She belongs solely to me."

As evening fell, Siddharth found himself aimlessly wandering near Arunima's house, his mind tangled in indecision. One moment, he yearned to enter her home once more, pouring out his love for her.

The next moment, doubt whispered that her love for him had faded away. Standing before her gate, he stood frozen, torn between conflicting directions. His ears perked up as the door creaked open, and he instinctively sidestepped, hiding behind the adjacent wall.

Arunima emerged, donning the pink and blue dress they had first encountered each other in, a sight that still held significance. She appeared beautiful, with a brown handbag slung over her left shoulder and her cell phone grasped tightly in her right hand.

Making her way towards a rickshaw, a thought crept into Siddharth's mind: "She's going to meet Saurabh." Jealousy surged within him, tempting him to intervene, yet he restrained himself, grappling with his emotions.

After about five hours:

It was midnight, and the doorbell disrupted Arunima's thoughts, leaving her wondering who could be visiting at such a late hour. Before she could fully process the situation, the doorbell rang for a second time, prompting her to hasten towards the door.

Curiosity and surprise mingled within her as she peered through the safety hole, only to discover Siddharth on the other side. "Siddharth!" she exclaimed, unable to contain her astonishment. she whispered to herself. "This late?"

With a mix of hesitation and concern, she opened the door, revealing Siddharth standing there, his demeanor void of any discernible emotion. No trace of anger or complaint tainted his expression.

"Hi Siddharth...come in," she invited, her voice tinged with a touch of uncertainty. "If my memory serves me right, you were supposed to depart tonight," Arunima pointed out, recalling their previous plans.

He remained silent, his silence speaking volumes.

"Siddharth?" Arunima's voice wavered, a hint of anxiety lacing her words.

"Yeah. Actually, I cancelled my flight," he replied, stepping inside. Arunima closed the door behind him. "I thought I would spend some time with you."

"Um, Siddharth... I believe I've already mentioned to you..." she started, uncertain of how to continue.

"I know, Arunima, and I'm sorry for the way I reacted. Forget about our affair, but we have been and will remain friends forever. So, can I spend some time with my friend?" he said with a sad smile. Arunima nodded, a flicker of relief crossing her face.

She prepared a cup of coffee for him and settled on the sofa opposite him. The atmosphere seemed more relaxed now, both of them finding solace in casual conversation.

"So, when can I meet the lucky guy?" Siddharth asked playfully.

"Who? Oh, Saurabh? Sure, whenever you are in Mumbai next time," Arunima replied.

"Why wait until next time, Arunima? Why not tomorrow? After all, I'll have to book a new ticket for myself. Let's check his availability and plan accordingly. What do you think?" Siddharth proposed eagerly.

"Siddharth..." Arunima hesitated, unsure of how to respond.

"Don't worry, I won't lay a finger on him," he chuckled. "Trust me, I just want to meet the person whom my best friend has chosen as her life partner," he added, his smile genuine.

"I understand, dear. Actually, Saurabh is currently out of town, which is why I mentioned next time. I'm truly sorry," Arunima explained, her voice tinged with apologetic regret.

"Hmm... okay. No issues. Chalo, at least show me a photo of him, yaar. Now, please don't come up with any more excuses, okay?" Siddharth requested, his tone light-hearted.

"Siddharth... I don't have any photo of him," she confessed, her conscience weighing heavy.

"And you expect me to believe that?" Siddharth challenged, raising an eyebrow.

"You have to, Siddharth," she pleaded softly.

"Okay. Now, tell me he's not on any of the social networking sites. Tell me, Arunima," he pressed, his gaze unwavering.

Her heart began to race, and she found herself unable to utter a single word.

Siddharth insisted, "Okay, give me his number. Let me speak to him."

Arunima hesitated, "Siddharth, it's too late to call him now."

Undeterred, Siddharth persisted, "No problem. I'll call him tomorrow morning. Give me his number."

Arunima remained silent, her gaze fixed on him, unable to provide a response.

Siddharth let out a sigh and began pacing the room, expressing his frustration, "This is unbelievable! My best friend is in love with someone who has no contact number, no social presence, and no photograph. How am I supposed to trust this?"

Drawing closer to Arunima, who remained seated on the sofa, Siddharth squatted down in front of her, his eyes searching for answers.

He asked in a serious tone, "Where did you go today evening, Arunima?"

Arunima stayed silent, unable to provide an answer.

Siddharth's anger surged as he confronted her, his voice growing more intense. "Will you tell me, or do I need to tell you?" His eyes blazed with intensity, and his temper flared.

Arunima stammered, her voice filled with fear, "Wh...what do you mean, Siddharth? How do you...?" A wave of unease washed over her.

Siddharth's frustration grew, and he continued, "Fine. If you won't tell me, I'll tell you instead. Arunima, I followed you this evening. I thought you were going to meet

Saurabh, but what I discovered was far from it."

Her heart pounded in her chest, but she remained silent, unable to utter a single word.

"Arunima..." Siddharth held her hands, his voice filled with a mix of sorrow and disbelief. "I always believed that we shared everything in our lives. I can't comprehend what I discovered today. How could you keep this illness from me? I always thought I held an important place in your life..." Tears welled up in his eyes.

Arunima's voice quivered as she responded, "Siddharth, you're not just an important part of my life... you're an integral part of who I am. I feel incomplete without you." Tears cascaded down her cheeks.

"Then why did you do this to me, my dear? Why?" Siddharth's voice cracked with anguish.

"I'm sorry, Siddharth... I know how deeply you love me, and I thought this news would shatter you. I believed that by parting ways, you could find a new love and not be burdened by my condition. I didn't want to leave you alone in this world," she sobbed, her words laced with regret.

"You can't leave me, Arunima. You're not going anywhere... I won't let you go," Siddharth declared, embracing her tightly as they both wept, their tears expressing the depth of their emotions.

Chapter 9

A Few Days of Joy

Leukemia, or blood cancer, has become a curable disease when diagnosed early. However, in Arunima's case, the absence of early symptoms had allowed her cancer to progress to an advanced stage without receiving timely treatment.

She was now faced with the devastating reality that she had only six months to live. Arunima was painfully aware of her limited time left, and Siddharth had just learned about her condition.

It was a somber and emotionally charged night as Siddharth and Arunima reunited after a long time, but their love had taken on a different meaning in the face of Arunima's illness.

Despite being under the care of one of the best doctors in the country, Siddharth insisted on seeking a second opinion to ensure Arunima's well-being. However, the results remained unchanged, and Arunima continued her treatment under the guidance of her initial doctor.

Arunima urged Siddharth to return to Delhi and resume his studies, emphasizing that she would be taken care of. But Siddharth refused to leave her side, accompanying her to her subsequent chemotherapy session. It was a difficult experience, but Siddharth resolved to remain emotionally strong, at least in front of Arunima.

In moments of solitude, he allowed himself to express his emotions, grappling with the guilt of not recognizing the extent of Arunima's suffering and misinterpreting her physical changes as mere superficialities. He struggled to forgive himself for failing to comprehend the depth of her pain while their love endured.

He remained there for a week before informing her that he would be leaving the following day. Arunima nodded in agreement, wanting him to resume his classes. Siddharth gazed at her, noticing her thinning hair and dark circles under her eyes. He tenderly planted a kiss on her forehead.

Locking eyes with Arunima, Siddharth's determination radiated from his gaze.

"Sweetie, you have 15 days remaining," he whispered softly.

Perplexed, Arunima asked, "Fifteen days remaining for what, Siddharth?"

He smiled gently. "I will return in 15 days and take you with me."

Arunima couldn't comprehend his words. "Take me where? Siddharth, I can't go anywhere..."

Siddharth interrupted, "You're an Indian girl, sweetheart. It's tradition for a married woman to leave her home and live with her husband."

A mix of emotions washed over Arunima's face. "Are you out of your mind? We can't get married."

Siddharth playfully teased, "Are you still in love with this Saurabh?"

Arunima shook her head, trying to gather her thoughts. "You're being ridiculous. I don't even have six months..."

Siddharth remained resolute. "So what? I don't care."

Concerned for his well-being, Arunima insisted, "I don't want you to be labeled as a widower, Siddharth. I want you to have a normal life with a loving partner."

Siddharth replied firmly, "And that's exactly what I'm doing, honey. I'm living my life with my partner, with you."

Arunima struggled to provide more reasons, but Siddharth's unwavering commitment to her and their love rendered her arguments futile. He wanted to shower her with the joys of life and take care of her in every possible way. Two weeks later, they got married, determined to be together until death do them part, cherishing the precious time they had left.

Chapter 10

Love's Farewell Symphony

In the days that followed, Siddharth and Arunima lived every moment as if it were their last. They embraced love and happiness, creating cherished memories together. Siddharth dedicated himself to making Arunima's remaining time as beautiful as possible, ensuring that her days were filled with laughter, joy, and comfort.

They traveled to picturesque destinations, holding hands and savoring the beauty of nature. They danced in the rain, feeling the drops on their faces and reveling in the simple pleasure of being alive.

They shared heartfelt conversations, expressing their deepest thoughts, dreams, and fears. Siddharth listened to Arunima's every word, etching them into his heart, while Arunima marveled at Siddharth's unwavering love and strength.

As Arunima's health gradually declined, Siddharth remained by her side, providing unwavering support and care. He held her when she felt weak, wiped away her tears, and whispered words of love and encouragement. Every day became a battle against time, but their love flourished amidst the pain and uncertainty.

In the final moments, surrounded by loved ones, Siddharth held Arunima's fragile hand, his eyes filled with love and sorrow. He gently brushed a strand of hair away from her face and planted a tender kiss on her forehead. With tears streaming down his cheeks, he whispered, "Thank you for teaching me the true meaning of love and for being my guiding light. You will always be in my heart."

Arunima mustered a weak smile, her eyes reflecting a profound sense of tranquility. "Thank you for loving me unconditionally, for demonstrating the power of your love, and for making my journey so beautiful. I will be watching over you, my love," she whispered, her words filled with a mixture of gratitude and farewell.

As Arunima's breathing grew faint, Siddharth held her close, cherishing their final embrace. In that moment, time stood still, and their souls intertwined, transcending the boundaries of life and death. With a gentle exhale, Arunima's spirit peacefully departed, leaving behind a legacy of love that would forever echo in Siddharth's heart.

Siddharth, though broken-hearted, found solace in the memories they shared, knowing that their love was eternal. He carried Arunima's essence within him, and her love continued to guide him through the darkest of days. Siddharth honored her memory by living a life filled with compassion, kindness, and a deep appreciation for every precious moment.

And so, their love story, marked by pain and loss, touched the hearts of those who heard it. It reminded them of the fragility of life, the power of love, and the importance of cherishing every fleeting moment. Siddharth and Arunima's love became a beacon of hope, inspiring others to embrace love, live fully, and treasure the gift of each passing day.

And as the tears flowed from the eyes of those who heard their story, a profound sense of gratitude welled up within them, reminding them of the preciousness of love and the beauty that can be found even in the face of heartbreaking loss. Siddharth and Arunima's love became immortal, an eternal flame that illuminated the path for all those seeking true and unconditional love.

And so, their love story, though marked by sorrow, became a testament to the enduring power of love and the beauty that can emerge from the depths of pain. It became a story that touched the hearts of many, reminding them to cherish love, live authentically, and find solace in the memories that will forever linger in their hearts.

In the depths of love's final sigh,
Two souls embraced, preparing to fly.
Their love's tale, an ethereal art,
A unique elegy, from heart to heart.

With whispered words and tender touch,
They bid farewell, but loved so much.
In the silence, a poignant grace,
A short elegy, in love's embrace.

No tears of sorrow, but tears of light,
As they embraced love's final night.
In unity, they found their peace,
A unique elegy, love's sweet release.

For in their parting, love did grow,
A bond unbroken, forever to show.

Though they departed, souls entwined,

A short elegy, their love defined.

In this unique elegy, love transcends,

Through words unwritten, it never ends.

A testament to love's lasting flame,

In whispered echoes, their love remains.

__END__